WALKING
A HAUNTED SANDBAR

WALKING

A SANDBAR:

A Suspense and Horror Collection

BY RORRY NIGHTTRAIN EAST

Photo of a stained glass window by bigevil600
Photo of a retro diner by Greg Hennigan
Photo of a rearview mirror by sunshinehunters.com

ACKNOWLEDGEMENTS

Dexter and Sandra Seay
of Silver City, N.M.

With a special thanks to
Debra Colbert and Essence
of Los Angeles, Calif.

FOREWORD

WALKING A SANDBAR:
A Suspense and Horror Collection

It's Alfred Hitchcock meets Edgar Allan Poe meets the Beatitudes: for "Wisdom is justified by her children," and her children were born to read another nightstand classic.

Rorry Nighttrain East
Silver City, New Mexico
March 25, 2015

TABLE of CONTENTS

WALKING
A HAUNTED SANDBAR

OLD SEA YARNS

Night fell fluidly with its phoenix sun in a flight of sudden disappearance, as if it were a bird on fire. Lately, though, the rebirth of my dreams has become complicated waters. They arrive earlier and earlier every night while walking a haunted sandbar.

Without proposing any definitive bathos, time is funny; it all seems to have begun at our historical clock tower. I cannot tell you our exact location, except to say we are on the east coast of United States in the hurricane zone, and it would ruin tourism to expose our seaside town to any further scrutiny—though I can say we have red, double-decker buses.

File it under the heading of Old Sea Yarns— if you will. It is still difficult to imagine how our unassuming cottage town upon a cliff had some-how hit the underbelly of time, and that there are soulless creatures wandering this earth in a modern age along littoral regions that somehow reminded one of a quaint English seaside city.

Most folks around this seasonal beach-town just call me Xanthus King, but Xanthus will do. I'm a bit of an amateur historian around these parts; when Wyatt Kolton came to see me fresh off his boat from Southampton about a hot newspaper article he was writing, I simply told him a few of the following sea yarns.

"So . . . you want to know the unofficial tale of limbo heights?" I forcefully asked my newspaper friend and new citizen.

"Definitely . . ." Wyatt insisted, with a thick British accent.

"Okay; a ship sank over on the point with great loss of life last year," I informed my new friend. "You arrived here about nine months later, and right about then, all the local folks began to clam-up because they didn't want to discourage the tourists with enervating sea yarns."

Wyatt asked, "Well . . . how did the vessel sink?"

"No one really knows," I replied. "All the findings were inconclusive."

"Then how many people perished?" the newsman patiently asked me.

"Maybe fifty," I said. "But first . . . let me tell you how it all happened, and I want you to keep this part on the down-low. There are heresy hunters who may want to string an old Christian like me up on high."

"Sure, sure . . ." Wyatt agreed.

I then told that smart reporter, "There is a wealthy man in town—Ulysses Vincent—do you know him?"

"Of course," Wyatt spoke out softly. "I haven't really met him in person but he owns the newspaper."

"All right; it gets a little weird here," I said,

"but Ulysses Vincent's son, Killian, and Tobias Marshall were both after the same girl, named Jody Willow London. Only, her father, Utah London, wouldn't let either man near his pride and joy. To cut to the chase—her drowning on that ship out on the point had to be foul play, by either one of the Londons or Tobias Marshall. It was one of those three men."

"I don't know . . ." Wyatt said, with an understandably puzzled look. "So . . . who or what is haunting this seaside paradise like the 'White Cliffs of Dover'?"

"It's 'Casket Lard' himself!" I boldly informed the curious reporter.

"What the heck is 'Casket Lard'?!" Wyatt moaned.

I said, "That's all that was left of those shipwrecked bodies that were retrieved. Their remains were only a rotten, lard-like substance by the time we got any outside help."

"That's bloody sickening!" Wyatt cried.

"Oh, it's worse than that," I said. "You can sometimes still smell the stench of their presence around here on a warm summer night."

"Casket Lard, huh?" Wyatt remarked.

"Yep," I said.

"All right then," Wyatt replied. "So where do I find out about getting some pictures of these 'Casket Lard' persons or things?"

"Don't worry about pictures," I said. "They'll be out and about tonight. It's the 'October Fest' event over at the old heinous clock tower, and those undead creatures will be staggering around along the cliffs."

Wyatt Kolton didn't take my advice. He passed on, going to festival of the cliffs near the 'Little Ben' clock tower. He went over to the only mortuary in town to interview our creepy-looking mortician instead.

It seems that every year Utah London held a special event for his deceased daughter called a 're-funeral.' The funeral director even explained to Wyatt that re-funerals were a lot like getting re-married, and since no one ever complained, the mortuary was more than glad to take the money.

"Excuse me, sir," Wyatt asked the attending mortician, "but what is 'Casket Lard?'"

"Oh, never speak of that!" The oddball mortician tried to brush the reporter off as he performed his exequies.

"Okay." Wyatt interrogated just a bit longer. "Then what can you tell me about the ship that sank last year — or any ghost sightings?"

"All I can tell you, my good man," the mortician whispered into Wyatt's ear, "shhhhh . . . but the ghosts play hide and seek in here at night."

"What ghosts?" the reporter questioned.

"Well, there's Jody Willow London's ghost and all the others," the creepy mortician insisted.

"Do you know of any other unusual events off-hand?" Wyatt asked, as the strange re-funeral service continued onward with a dark-sounding organ march.

"Uh, yes . . ." the funeral director admitted. "In the mornings when we open up, we can still smell the stench of the sunken Captain Dalton's ghost and the temperature is very cold."

Wyatt returned to my modest cottage above the sea that same evening. He wanted to know why I had always walked the haunted sandbars. He also wanted my advice on how to bring Mr. Utah London out of his reclusive shell.

"Xanthus . . .? Can you tell me anything about Utah London having all these strange re-funerals?"

"Mr. London thinks his daughter is still alive!" Xanthus exclaimed

"Why would he think something like that?" Wyatt inquired as we watched the long, serene wind roll into the shore below the lofty cliffs. "I don't get it."

"Because Mr. London's daughter and several others around here have not made amends to their final pillow," the clear-headed Xanthus replied.

"What final pillow?" The stunned reporter asked with fealty.

"The second-death, my son . . ."

Wyatt then begged, "You mean, she's still alive?"

"I don't know exactly what Jodie Willow London is!" Xanthus admitted. "Though, I know someone is somehow prolonging her unwanted stay above the ground."

It wasn't until about his third or fourth return to the cottage that my new friend the newsman took a much more serious tone. Wyatt now insisted that I come clean with the full story.

"Xanthus, I need to know why you are always walking that haunted sandbar—especially a low tide."

"Because they are not afraid of me! Don't you know that this entire town is an ancient cult?"

"What kind of ancient cult?"

Xanthus said, "Do you know of any other town that has re-funerals?!"

"N-no," Wyatt's words stumbled to eschew anything unlucky.

"Forget about all these crazy people," Xanthus croaked. "Just get out of town while you still can. These so-called esoteric people sacrifice at least one ship a year and then blame it on the 'Devil's Triangle,' and no one questions it. And, last year, they inauspiciously sacrificed the cult leader's daughter for their one-hundredth year anniversary."

"Why didn't I catch on to all of this sooner?" Wyatt asked with a torn look upon his face.

"It's not your fault," Xanthus said. "It's because you always mind your own business and you're a basic homebody. But believe me: some of those creatures have not slept in centuries . . ."

"So why do you walk those haunted sand-bars?"

"Because most of the creatures drowned in the sea hundreds of years ago and they are afraid of low tide."

"Why low tide?" the reporter asked.

"That's when the main cult leaders throw their unsuspecting rejects back into the ocean for their second-death . . ."

"What if I try to join their cult, under false pretenses?" Wyatt questioned his real-human mentor.

Xanthus said, "They would only drown you first and let your body remain underwater until you became one of the 'Casket Lard' cult. Wait! I hear them coming up the hill—let's get down to the seashore before they reach us . . ."

After being followed down to the beach, the once-disguised bodies of the cult had shed their outer, human skins, as Wyatt and I were cornered near the sand dunes under a pale, shifting moonlight.

Those creatures were now horrible globs of thick, white grease that dripped as they staggered toward us. They were carrying Miss London's unforgiving-urn toward the sea for her second death, after a re-funeral; as her two former suitors who were normal and human-men themselves began to push the 'Casket Lard' cult out into the waves from behind. Everyone covered their eyes as the ocean waters lit up with a fantastic, electric-blue shine, for a moment, until the creatures all wept as they were expunged of their spirits and concupiscent energies for infinity. It was an intense death that even Neptune would have honored—were he a true being.

"As sea yarns go," said my newspaper friend while we watched new people fervidly moving back into our peaceful and dream-like town, "boy gets girl—girl gets two boys for the price of one, because her two suitors shard her ashes whenever the mortician gives Tobias Marshall and Killian an extra new urn."

"Nothing like a happy ending," Wyatt said, with a funny smirk.

"I'll just forget you said that," Xanthus replied as the two began walking a haunted sandbar with a fulsome cheer.

Meanwhile . . . over at the mortuary on the other side of the town, the mortician was cheerfully getting ready for his last funeral—before his retirement—and out popped the cult leader, Utah London, a half-human and a half-Casket Lard creature. A morbid organ song began to play onward as the creature smothered the undertaker until dead on the edge of a gaudy and empty coffin, and then he turned around, dripping of a foul, casket-lard grease, while

looking for any readers of this book, as he said,
"NEXT . . ."

Hope is
the bellwether spirit
for a victory to glory
temperament.

PUSHBUTTON EXECUTIONS

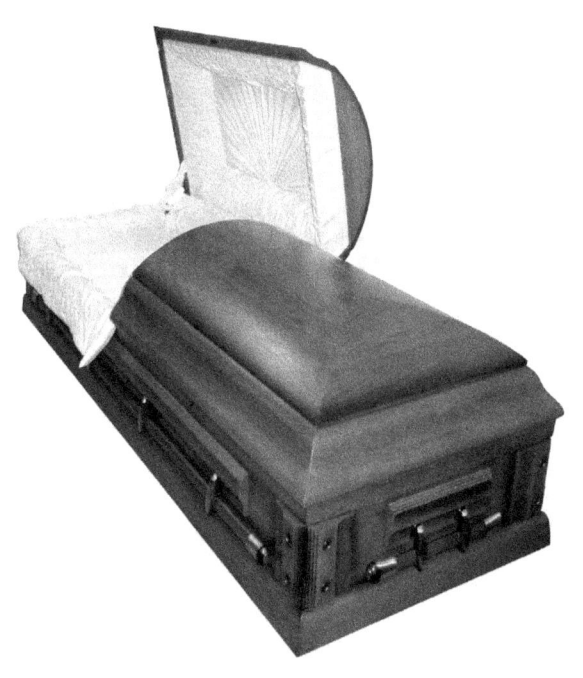

One
casket door
closes,
and another
can of worms
opens.

PUSHBUTTON EXECUTIONS

You may call me Mr. Sage. A multitude of people have joked around about my fitting name, but it is Xavier Sage—when sounded correctly. I am neither a psychic nor a mystic of any kind. I simply make educated guesses with a very high percentage of human success.

One of my former clients, by the name of Sean Heath, once came to me about his half-brother on Death Row, asking about the future of the American "death penalty."

"I completely and utterly disagree with anything as hateful as human executions," I compassionately told him. "I also want you to know that all future jails will be closed down, and unfortunately men and women will be implanted with a device called 'The Judge': a machine that does not season its judgments with love."

"I don't get it," Sean replied. "That sounds even worse than now."

"Yes, it's a sad-commentary on our species . . ." I said. "'The Judge' will follow anyone even suspected of a crime, and, if it determines that an infraction of the law has occurred, that ominous device will even cripple a human being with its electrodes. So be especially wary if a real felony is ever committed; a person will be instantly frozen-solid right where they stand in their final tracks. Then, if the mainframe and/or two or more operators find you guilty—you'll be boiled down into a soup, from a block of ice, and removed from the city streets."

"That's an instant pushbutton execution," Sean exclaimed.

"Yes," I said, "and . . . that's not even the worst of it. One's human-remains will be sent in sludge piles of watery soup to feed the government-owned livestock ranches, and even innocent people will all thus be secondhand-cannibals."

"That's just awful," Sean cried.

"Hey, that's not even the worst of it . . ." I insisted. "There will be colossal glitches in that morbid system, whereupon innocent people will be accidently killed—just like nowadays!"

Sean said, "Then I guess it just gets worse for people, or it somehow stays the same?"

"What do you expect when man is always trying to play God?"

"I expect J-U-S-T-I-C-E," Sean moaned.

"Well . . . I dread to give you the bad news," I said with a deep sigh, "but sometimes 'Justice' . . . is JUST ICE . . ."

"I'm almost sorry that I even asked you about my half-brother's situation, Mr. Sage."

"That's perfectly okay," I replied. "I'm especially sorry to have to tell you that mankind is such a screw-up that there is about a 70% probability some crazy terrorists will kidnap 'The Judge' network, and then send us all back into our caves to live like the apes well east of Eden."

Duped by Darwin, the Executioners all go ape, yet the survival of his misfit story depends on sour grapes. Power-hungry—amoral too—he thinks of mankind as a zoo; oh . . . exploited by Darwin's fishy philosophy (a would-be, bogus god), except for the very fact: his ideas are a stinking cod.

THE MIRROR
THAT WOULDN'T
LOOK BACK

ONE
SILENCER NIGHT

"It was the night before Christmas
and all through our . . . abode . . .
a man with his hit-list, and hood
MASK, NOW STRODE . . ."

But wait! The reason I became a hitman in the first place was so I might be able to work my own hours and be my own boss — to rid this world of a few questionable people on Santa's naughty list. Then I'd neatly send them to that good ol' Eternal Twenty-Winks Mortuary for an eternity to eternity time-out.

Sure . . . a few discerning people might even say that I'm the bad guy in this scenario, and of course I am, though we'll just let Santa work that out for himself through his own holiday maledictions. Let's just say my job was a major stumbling block.

It all started last year around the holidays, when my wife bought an unusual antique mirror inside a golden, scrolled, hand-held carrying case, only a few inches long. Before I knew it, our house burnt down, the wife and kids left me, I lost my good job as a grocery store butcher, and let's even say . . . I felt like a power-broker of stupidity without any universal truth in my life.

By the way, I'm Gunthor, and you might even say that I was so down, that the devil in the overheated apartment up above thought I was just another social-climber, when I screamed out my basement window: "I SURELY HATE EVERYONE . . . EQUALLY!"

"Do you . . .?!" my drunken/bum roommate asked me. "Say, with an attitude like that, I think I can get you a job as an exterminator."

Well, before I knew it, I was not only an exterminator; I was a hitman for a pest control company. The clincher was, they had me putting chemicals of death in unsuspecting people's drinks at a bar called The Last Watering Hole. The big boss didn't tell me I was using poison until I had already killed eighty-six stiffs. He said it was a knock-out potion. All things being unethically equal, I simply decided to start using a gun. At the time, it may have been a rationalization, but the big boss Mr. Raseac (which is 'Caesar' backward) had just forced me to work my last holiday season free of charge from sunset Halloween night, until noon Christmas day or he'd turn me in to the cops.

In my first nine years as a hitman, I wacked

so many people on Halloween night that this particular exterminator called it my "Deja Boo" evening; I always wore the same Halloween costume year after year. It was a blithesome event. I didn't see my own brokenness in a fallen world.

It was on a final Halloween job, just this holiday season, when I shot two men in pumpkin suits and one Cinderella. Sadly, I was contracted for just pumpkin-man, but another pumpkin guy and his Cinderella date saw me, so it was TRICK-rather-than-treat for all three of them. My odious repeater had spoken.

That's my crash course in "Death 101:" Keep the morticians busy, and remember, we are all only six feet away from owning permanent real estate, because the earth is under a curse called the "the death cycle." A world where right is wrong and wrong is right.

It was on my way home from that messy job that I realized the big boss was having me tailed. "Excuse me," a man in another skeleton suit asked me. "Do you have a light?"

"Sorry . . ." I said, "I don't smoke."

"Well, you just smoked three people back there," the other rude skeleton insisted with piercing eyes.

"You're wrong!" I replied.

"Why?" my opponent asked.

"Make that FOUR—sucker," I argued, as my auto-pistol then went . . . "PFFFFT . . . PFFFFT" with a bullet to his mastoid and one to his heart.

Class dismissed. I had failed God.

That other skeleton wasn't even my last job of the evening. I had a Marilyn Manroe job on the other side of Santa Clara valley. The only reason they wanted me to do the bad deed on 'Sleeping-Pill Beauty' . . . was . . . that I'd become a chemical-exit mechanic of high esteem in their own era of misguided tolerance.

Thanksgiving, as it is with too many families, can be a royal, blindfolded firing squad get-together. Thus, it was no surprise that my pushy, big boss sent me to crash the turkey day party of some journalist who'd pulled his racketeer covers in a negative story about his computer-scam enterprises . . .

"Good to have you here this evening, sir." A clueless doorman took my fake reservation.

"I'm here to see the big turkey," I jested as I wrestled with something other than flesh and blood.

"Oh, Baird Warren, 'the-scribe,' is in the living room with the rest of his poison pen pals . . ."

Talk about your "Silencer Night"; my job was to lure Baird Warren to any back room and hang him with his own belt—and definitely make it look like a suicide—but I was sick and tired of being lousy, old "Beelzebub's" grim reaper for wayward souls who rocked the boat. My officious gun was taking its toll with its single barrel and double-mindedness.

Therefore, I purposely screwed the job by food poisoning the entire party of twenty-five guests, and I left Baird Warren alive, all while planting damaging evidence behind, just to torque my boss off. Then I went to the big boss' house on Meridian Ave. in San Jose, California, with milk and cookies:

> "It was the night before Christmas
> and all through the . . . house . . .
> I then found the control-freak,
> MY BOSS, AND A LOUSE . . ."

"I've got a great present for you, boss," I shouted, while standing over his bed with a black silencer in Mr. Raseac's ugly face. "Aren't you just dying to see what Santa brought you?"

"Well . . . the caliber of your giving astounds me," the big boss mocked my words. "It's a very nice present, but look outside this house."

"Why?!"

"You are surrounded by fifty Santas with machine guns pointed right at you, Gunthor!"

"Not a problem, boss—I have brought my 'crowd pleaser' with me tonight."

"What's that?" the snotty boss asked.

"A small nuclear device." This happy Gunthor sighed, as I then shot him in the mid-stream of our conversation. "I also have a pre-dug escape tunnel leading to a gateway vehicle down in the government's 37th-parallel highway, leading clear across the U.S.A. underground. Enough of this 'health-and-wealth stuff'; I'm forced to do one more job—then I'm going to find me a new congregation with sound doctrine and out of the goodness of its heart will rebuke the devil's church of hitmen."

"The person in the mirror can read your mind .
Can you make eye contact?"
- Kamil Ali

None
are abandoned
by God;
it is just that
a soul can feel
alone and troubled
while on our way
from chaos to
a Higher order.

TWO
THE DINER FROM SPACE

Shelley was the second owner of the ominous, gold-encased mirror. She found it in a used car's glove compartment of the previous hitman's escape vehicle.

From all reports, pallid, blonde Shelly had a very special experience with the mirror of dire wishes and contorted dreams, like no other.

On a long, lonely trip out in the sticks of New Mexico's rural towns, Shelley began to let her sleepless eyes drift off a tumbleweed-lined highway in the darkness, until she mawkishly caught a sudden glimpse of an upcoming diner — the only lights for miles and miles. She turned the wheel and pulled to a hesitant stop with a farrago mixture of hand signals and mirror play.

Initially, she hadn't noticed how streamlined the low-profile building was, nor how it sat oddly tilted. Shelly was just flat-tired, and she only wanted to check her make-up with her newly-attained and pleasant-looking mirror; then she hurried inside the diner for some coffee. It was 2 a.m., and not a single car was on the eerily-quiet highway. She was the only customer in the diner, too.

"I'm surprised you guys are open this late," Shelley exclaimed as she sat alone in a booth. "Just . . . coffee, please."

"Yes, earth-ma'am," a strange-looking waitress addressed her.

"Oh," Shelley laughed, "I get it—your diner has a futuristic space theme to it."

"Would you like to view our 'Invasion Special'?" The weird waitress asked in a maladroit tone.

Shelley said, "Wow . . . you guys are out of this world."

"You may be certain of that, earth-ma'am." The male cook chuckled from behind the counter.

"I left California the other day and I'm afraid I've lost my way," Shelley said with a slight yawn. "Do you know how to get to Roswell from here?"

"We live in Roswell," the waitress replied as she nodded over at the unusual-looking cook in space garb.

"What are you guys doing way out here in the middle of nowhere?" Shelly inquired.

"We like open spaces," the strange cook remarked. "We are both pilots . . ."

"No kidding?" Shelley said, "What do you like to fly?"

"Mostly, experimental aircraft . . ." the waitress sang as she poured more black liquid into Shelley's cup. "So how do you like our interstellar brew?" her miscreant voice rang.

"It's the best." Shelley sighed. "You know — when I was just a kid, we used to go to a diner in Fresno called Mars."

"We've both been there," the cook announced. "In fact — we own that property!"

"No? You own Mars?" the customer said.

"Yes — of course, we'll show you our deed," the minatory cook exclaimed. "Please put your safety-belts on . . ."

"Wait, I mean . . . is this a joke??" Shelley screamed and began to lour as she buckled up with a pair of hidden straps.

The spinning, silver spacecraft lifted off, and it was gone in a streak of light toward the red planet of war, so very far from earth. The country sheriff found Shelley's car the next morning, while the only thing he found was a small, gold mirror on her front seat to attest to her sudden vanishing.

"It's called the Infinity Effect."
- Edward M. Wolfe

To walk
in the Spirit
is to skip
a stale moment.

THREE
LOOKING FORWARD IN A REARVIEW MIRROR

Illinois was the tow truck driver's name. He'd helped to impound Shelley's car, and both the car and its mirror became his, at auction. It was such a good deal at only two-hundred dollars that Illinois took one quick look into that nonthreatening mirror and he put on his best overalls to visit the local bar for a night of serious drinking. The party night was so serious, in fact, that Illinois offered the bartender his new antique, handheld mirror in trade for six more shots of whiskey; but the kicker was . . . they both closed the bar down and had a high-speed motorcycle race for the title of Illinois' new car. Café racing was Illinois' true métier.

The race was to be from the bar in Roswell, New Mexico to the Big Sur—California's Bixby Bridge—above the shimmering, blue Pacific

Ocean.

Unfortunately, when Illinois arrived in Big Sur, the café racer-bartender was no longer to be found behind him, after being lost somewhere on the winding hills of Pacheo Pass, California, not much more than one-hundred miles from the ocean.

It seems the bartender gave his newly-attained compact golden mirror to a woman named Sookie at a Union 76 gas station when he ran out of gas money for his motorcycle race. It was a crippling setback, but Sookie gave the failed racer her own brown-bag lunch, which consisted of two sandwiches and a one-hundred dollar bill, to get him back to his Roswell bar.

"Are you confused as to which way is home?" Sookie asked the bothered racer as he put air in his tires.

"Nope," he replied. "I'm just wondering which way Reality is . . ."

"You can't get there from here." Sookie laughed.

"So what are you going to do with the fancy, golden mirror that you took in on trade?" he called over to her as he topped off his tank.

"I think I'll use it to neither confirm nor deny that I'm beautiful." She laughed again, and the bartender sped away in the dust.

It didn't take but a day or two until a sneaky criminal came into Sookie's gas station and he stole her valuable mirror right off the countertop when she wasn't looking.

All the while—Illinois had remained at the finish line in Big Sur, where he'd decided to take a mini vacation. Yet the mirror's powers were never passed on to the bartender: Illinois was backing his motorcycle up, on a high, Big Sur cliff, and he fell backwards several hundred feet to his demise; because the mirror's curse had reverted back to him!

Our next heartbeat
is from God:
We are on His
time schedule,
and that means
self-justification
is already
out-of-date.

FOUR
THE ROLODEX OF FUTURE ASSASSINATIONS

That same sneaky criminal who'd stolen the golden-case mirror from the gas station counter, took one look inside it, and he traded the hand-held antique for a slightly-used Rolodex at the nearest storage-locker sale.

When Rike, the mirror-thief, returned to his seedy hotel in Salinas, he started going through the used Rolodex files and he stopped at the letter "K."

It was written out as "Kennedy" . . . Dealey Plaza, grassy knoll Dallas, Texas—November 1963 . . . only the card had been pre-dated for the earlier date of November 1960. (That was two years before the assassination.)

Rike just laughed it off as some kind of a teenager's idea of a prank—until he saw the names "Regan" and "Ford" under the term "attempted."

He was obviously flabbergasted, though Rike continued to research a few presidential-sounding names he'd never heard before.

Every door
to grace
has a sign,
and on the
other side
a wonder.

Of what, Rike didn't know; he had been adopted and grown up in a dozen different foster homes, but they had never told him his native-born last name. He'd been a twin brother separated at birth. The last name was "Raseac," which meant Caesar when read backwards.

Instantly, Rike came across the name "Raseac" while he was busy thinking about how he'd recently become president of his own "Thief Guild" ring after being promoted by all the local crooks and fences.

It was only then that a man named Gunthor fired two bullets into Rike's head from his own fire escape, and his grim reaper had come like a thief in the daylight.

The indomitable mirror had won again.

"The mirror is the worst judge of true beauty."
- Sophia Nam

FIVE
THE DAY REFRIGERATORS TOOK OVER THE EARTH

A few machines defy the human imagination. Some of them warm us, and others leave us feeling somewhat cool.

Detective Emerson Aries was investigating two different cases on that unforgettable night that he first heard the refrigerators had taken over. Firstly, he had the murder of a thief, via two bullets from his fire-escape window; then, he had the rumor about the hundreds of refrigerators that were supposedly stumbling down the city streets of his hometown, Seattle, and blocking every roadway that led toward Alaska. He couldn't wait to get back home and break the case wide open.

Detective Aries was consulting on another case in California, and just when he'd looked into a golden mirror, which was his only clue, abnormal events in his hometown had begun to happen.

He'd been searching for a clue in that remarkable mirror's case, and now he had no clue at all as to why average citizens were now calling police stations up and down the west coast so frantically with questions like, "Is your refrigerator running?"

Needless to say, Detective Aires was clever enough to return home and stop that disturbing march of the refrigerators by realizing that the cursed mirror had something to do with it all.

It took weeks to clear the cluttered and Freon-lined streets, and hundreds of stumbling refrigerators made it up to Alaska, as well.

I should know, because about fifty of them blocked the freeway onramps while marching slowly past my Seattle-based antique shop. In fact—it was Detective Aires who brought the dangerous and scornful mirror to me. He's so famous for stopping the refrigerator march that everyone now calls him "Seattle's son in the rain."

Uh-huh, he'd even figured out that the refrigerators were only marching on their way, in a voodoo-trance fashion, up to Alaska—just to chill for a while.

"The mirror will only lie when you look at it
through a mask."
- Anthony Liccione

SIX
A BROKEN
POETIC-DEVICE

Call me Mr. Xue, as my true identity must remain anonymous for security purposes; although, I still watch onward with a somewhat tilted-head at such a tiny, powerful, golden box. It has been nothing short of a Peddler of Grievance for far too many years. I am also quite glad that it is now broken. I dropped the mirror in my shop, and it broke into a strange, spider-web pattern the other day.

There shall never be another of its kind. That obscure and innocent-looking mirror held too many blameless human beings in its web of captive limbo and otherworldly charms. I have locked it away in a special vault with the strictest instructions to have to have the mirror buried below my family's crypt upon the day of my death. It is far too much of a golden beast for anyone else to gaze into its golden frame again. That is why you may only refer to me as Mr. Xue.

No one knows where that "Inventions of Invention Itself" originated from. No one. And none shall know where it has gone: "as far as the east is from the west."

Notwithstanding, we are all mirrors unto each other . . . look at me . . . What would be your reflection in the face of knowing that such unbearable forces still exist . . .?

We cannot stand against the powers of darkness on our own. Its schemes are too numerable. Ever wonder why things just don't seem to work out? Maybe we need to move from a place, where we are only tolerated, into a place of love. Strangely enough—even America was founded on a church-relocation project.

"Tension is the Mirror of the Past."
- Saab

CITY OF SKELETONS

CITY OF SKELETONS

We all battle the same demons, except when such lecherous things are gone, and then all that is left is a city of skeletons.

It is a great emptiness in the night to be alone within a sleeping city; there are about 40,000 suicides per year in U.S.A., but where do they go?

Sometimes I think they've merely inhabited their own city of skeletons, for far too long. They've gone to adapt to their infinite choices of self-crucifixion. Almost none of them are cowards. There is a cachet to such human feelings. Even though wrong.

Griffin Chase awoke from his throes of insomnia at exactly 3 a.m., as usual, so he decided to get dressed and take a brisk walk through the park. The city lights were blinking yellow off and on at the first intersection as he rushed and tried to tire himself, and Griffin couldn't help but notice a car across the street with its door flung open and a skeleton arm leaning onto the street.

There was absolutely no one in sight as Griffin jogged two more city blocks down Sacramento Street to a parked police car, and to his astonishment there were two skeletons in the front seat, both in police uniforms with bony-white, empty eye sockets and pearly-white teeth.

Griffin started looking inside buildings as he jogged even farther down the empty streets at a faster pace, and he found an all-night coffee shop with a long row of skeleton men and women all seated on stools at the counter — and they were definitely dead.

"What the dubious-Darwin is going on here?" Griffin asked himself in a loud roar. But there was no answer. He now knew that he was in a city of the dead. Griffin turned, and he ran back homeward as fast as he could to take a couple sleeping pills that had been prescribed to him by another saw bones; and he finally fell fast asleep. He'd found that sure dichotomy between life and death.

Nine hours later, Griffin awoke to the noises of a crowded and clamoring city. He turned his TV set on to the news station and watched two more talking dead-heads spew their grave words of more war, then he turned it off and ran out to the street to see a crowd of low-consciousness people arguing over mere pettiness itself.

"Oh, that's right . . ." Griffin told himself as he strolled on toward work, where his cruel boss was waiting to scold him as usual. "I've always lived in a city of skeletons. I won't take them seriously anymore. It's time to love the hell out of them."

Purpose
is the oxygen
of human existence,
and Achievement is
its more learned
older brother.

BOOKS BY RORRY NIGHTTRAIN EAST

Passengers of Meandering Dream
The Night is a Panther
In the Gliding Sudden
August Messenger
Eventide Crows
Two Ships Passing in the Desert
The Sixth Oath To The Winds
The Vacant City and other Unusual Tales
Drastic Men of Clay
Runaway, Like a Dying Moon
Rob Tomb's Reality
A Tarantula's Dance in the Sun
Book in a Straitjacket
Barefoot Zeniths
Dents on A Fresno's Child
He Fell For Her .38's
Higher Than A Shoulder's Ceiling
Forevermore and Lately
A Pocketful of Always
The Grist Mills of Unlimited Being
The Wafture of a Thousand Echoes
Immortal Tales of the Vampire's Dentist
The Sea Walker

BOOKS BY RORRY
NIGHTTRAIN EAST (CONT'D)

The Soaring Never
Vermilion Wayfarers in the Rain
Doors Onto the Interior Rooms
The Hands in a Jar of Stars
The Mind Control Clock
Walking a Haunted Sandbar

ABOUT THE AUTHOR

Rorry Nighttrain East (a.k.a., R.L. Farr) is truly a literary anomaly. At least, he's really not some kind of author to typecast, nor even place into any single mode or genre. For he seems to run all gamuts of poetry & prose, humor, short stories, screenplays, teleplays, and even novels. What's next from this versatile new talent?

He says he writes because he's handicapped; and we believe him: Laugh, cry . . . and then wipe the tears away. You've found yourself the pen pal of a lifetime. (With two artificial legs thrown in, to boot.) A repentant, imperfect Christian still under construction.

Born on July 18, 1952 in Fresno, California, he is an alumnus of De Anza College Cupertino, California and was formerly a journeyman automobile mechanic for a Lincoln Mercury dealership in San Jose, California.

He has since moved from the "Golden State" and now lives upon a sprawling ranch where he writes just outside the beautiful, mile-high mountains of Silver City, New Mexico.

ABOUT THE BOOK

A lyrical yarn about an overly-curious
newspaper man transplanted from England
to the eastern coast of the USA, who stumbles
onto the fact that a one-hundred-year-old
cult of drowned sailors has complete control
of his quaint, seaside town.

A legend about a hand-held golden
mirror (with a portable vortex inside
its case); as it is randomly
passed between owners in separate
vignettes to change their lives
beyond human comprehension.

The ennui and general apathy of
living in a sleepless big city
that doesn't seem to care — as
expressed in skeleton symbols.

A humble man with great calculating
abilities uses his natural mind to
auto-suggest (the future of law and
order) hundreds of years from now.

RIVERSHORE BOOKS

www.rivershorebooks.com
blog.rivershorebooks.com
www.facebook.com/rivershore.books
www.twitter.com/rivershorebooks
Info@rivershorebooks.com